Not green-skinned, bulgey-eyed, bloodsucking monster scary.

Edwin Page was just plain scary.

It was all because of his hair. It was blacker than a bin bag full of bad dreams and that is what people saw. They looked at Scary Edwin Page's hair and felt like they were about to be dragged, screaming, into the darkest of nightmares.

Even dogs would whimper
and cower when Scary Edwin
Page walked by, and cats would spit and
run up trees. If a hamster had escaped
from its cage, it soon scampered back
when it saw Scary Edwin Page.

Scary Edwin Page liked being scary, but on one particular night each year Scary Edwin Page was very, very scary indeed and that night was Hallowe'en.

Scary Edwin Page would trick or treat around his town and people were so scared of him that he would collect enough sweets to last him for the rest of the year.

Every house was the same.
Scary Edwin Page would knock on a door,
the door would open and he would say...

"Trick or treat?"

The people would see his nightmarish
hair, throw all their sweets out to get
rid of him, slam their door shut,
lock it and hide behind the sofa.

This Hallowe'en was different. Word soon got around that Scary Edwin Page was 'Trick or Treating', so everyone in town turned out their lights and pretended not to be at home when he knocked on their doors. It didn't bother Scary Edwin Page...

...his treat sack was already so full it was almost splitting. He was about to go home when he saw a single light coming from an old house at the edge of town.

"Strange", thought Scary Edwin Page.
"I thought that house was empty.
Must be new people."
"New victims," he muttered to himself.
So Scary Edwin Page walked to the
house and knocked on the door.

There was no answer,
so he knocked again.

This time he heard soft
footsteps getting nearer and nearer
and eventually, with a long, moaning
creak, the door opened and there stood...

... an old lady.

"Trick or treat?"

hissed Scary Edwin Page through
his teeth as he grinned wickedly.

"Trick or treat?" smiled the old lady sweetly.
"Oooh, I do love choices."

"Errr..." said Scary Edwin Page.

"My, what lovely hair you've got!"
said the old lady.

"Umm..." said Scary Edwin Page.

"Ah, yes," said the old lady.
"Trick or treat wasn't it?
Okay, I choose trick..."

The old lady reached up her right
hand and grabbed her hair.
For a while, she looked a little puzzled
as she twisted and tugged at her hair,
this way and that. Then she smiled.
"Silly old me," she sighed.
"I remember now!"

Then, with the sucking sound
a Wellington boot makes when
it is pulled out of thick, gooey mud,
and the r-r-r-r-rip of dry paper…

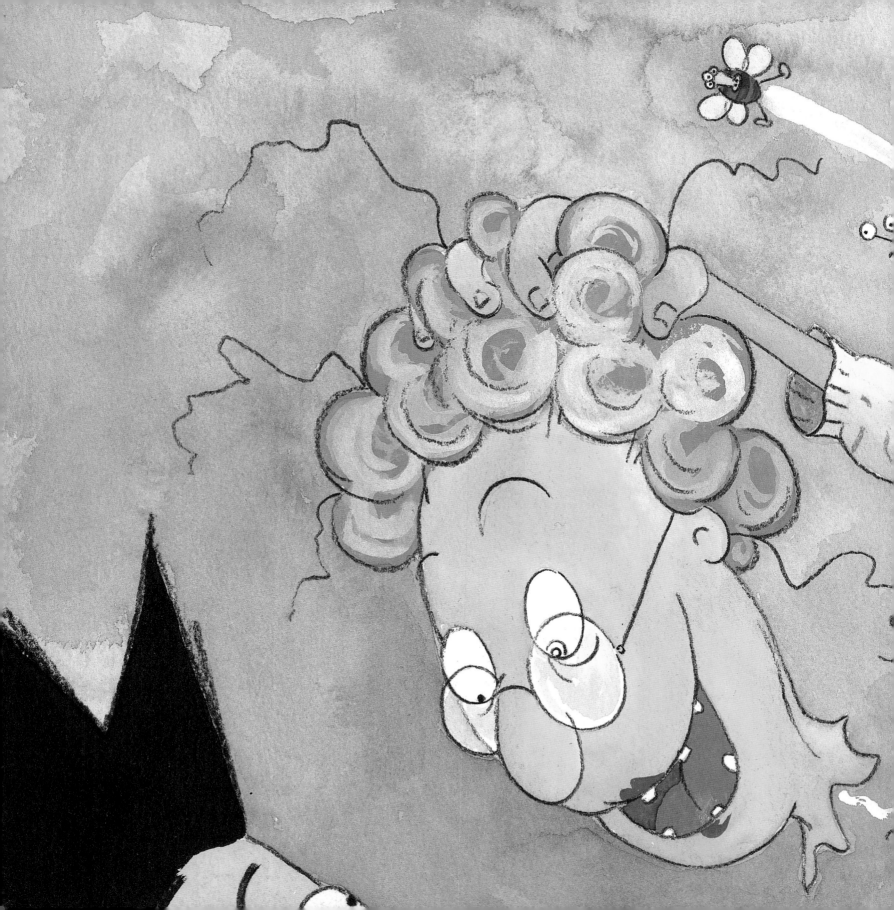

Scary Edwin Page ran and ran as fast as he could, dropping his bulging sack of treats so it didn't slow him down. He ran away from the sinister old house; he ran through the town with no lights on; he ran up the path to his house; he ran through his front door; he ran up the stairs and he ran, (well jumped) into his bed.

And he stayed hidden there, under the covers, shaking with fear, until morning.

Some people wonder how Scary... (sorry)...
Not-So-Scary Edwin Page's hair
changed colour that Hallowe'en but,
I think you'll agree, sometimes
it is better not to know...

For four truly scary boys,

Alec, Jamie, Brandon, Jake
and the 'real' Edwin Page,
who is not scary at all...
unless he is talking
about George.

A.S

For Bruno Bingley

D.P

First published in 2004
by Meadowside Children's Books
185 Fleet Street, London EC4A 2HS

Text © Alec Sillifant 2004
Illustrations © Daniel Postgate 2004
The rights of Alec Sillifant and Daniel Postgate
to be identified as the author and illustrator
have been asserted by them in accordance with
the Copyright, Designs and Patents Act, 1988.

A CIP catalogue record for this book
is available from the British Library.
10 9 8 7 6 5 4 3 2
Printed in China